BONJOUR,
PARIS!

This edition published by Parragon Books Ltd in 2015

Parragon Books Ltd
Chartist House
15–17 Trim Street
Bath BA1 1HA, UK
www.parragon.com

ISBN 978-1-4723-8234-4

Printed in China

MINNIE
IN
PARIS

Written by
SHEILA SWEENY HIGGINSON

Illustrated by
MIKE WALL

PaRragon

Bath · New York · Cologne · Melbourne · Delhi
Hong Kong · Shenzhen · Singapore · Amsterdam

It's Fashion Week in **PARiS!**

All the top designers are busy preparing for their shows.

And Minnie has been invited to go
to one of the shows.

THE HOUSE OF
CUCKOO CHANEL

Mademoiselle Minerva Mouse

You have been
invited to show your bows
at our Fashion Week event
in Paris, France.

"Ooh la la!
says Cuckoo-Loca.

"Your bows will be the hit of the runway!" Daisy cheers.

"**Paris!** Oh, my," Minnie sighs. "Every bow will

need to have style. Every bow will need to have flair."

Minnie designs a new
series of fashionable bows.

Daisy and Cuckoo-Loca **snip...**

and **staple...**

and **sew.**

Everything is ready – just in the nick of time.

Millie and Melody grab the biggest suitcase they can find.

Minnie and her crew race to the airport.

Look who else is going to Paris ...

Penguini the Magnificent!

"Have a **magical** day!" Minnie calls

to him as she chases after Millie and Melody.

Finally, it's time to take off!

The plane soars over the ocean ...

... and lands in France.

Daisy grabs the suitcase.

Cuckoo-Loca hails a taxi.

Minnie checks into the hotel,

and Millie and Melody find the room.

Uh-oh!

Daisy must have picked up Penguini's suitcase by mistake.

Now Minnie has no bows for the fashion show!

This is a

BOW-TASTROPHE!

One by one, Penguini's
bunnies hop out of the suitcase.

"Don't open that door!" Minnie says to her nieces.

But it's too late. The bunnies are gone!

"We'll round up the bunnies," Minnie says.

"Daisy, you and Cuckoo-Loca find

some ribbon. We need to make new bows."

Millie and Melody chase
one bunny down a busy street.

"Look, girls! It's the

Arc de Triomphe!"

Minnie calls.

Millie and Melody follow two bunnies onto a riverboat.

"The Seine River!" sighs Minnie.

"NOTRE-DAME CATHEDRAL!"

Minnie gasps. *"C'est magnifique!"*

Three bunnies scamper through a crowd of tourists.

Millie, Melody and Minnie chase after them.

"Should we go to help them, Daisy?" Cuckoo-Loca asks.

"It looks like Minnie and the girls are doing fine," Daisy says.

"There's one more shop we need to visit, anyway."

The girls find four bunnies in a field of flowers at the

Garden of Tulips.

"Oh, my," says Minnie. "These colours are

like the beautiful paintings inside the museum."

Melody and Millie go inside the museum
and run down the hall after five bunnies.

THE LOUVRE!

THE
MINNIE LISA

"I've always wanted to see the *Minnie Lisa*," says Minnie
to her nieces, as she gets a quick look at the famous painting.

Six bunnies crash into a cart
of croissants.

"Bon appétit!"

Minnie calls, taking one last bite of her omelette.

Seven bunnies pile onto a puppet-filled stage.

"What merry marionettes!"

Minnie applauds. "Now get those bunnies, girls!"

Minnie and her nieces tiptoe after eight bunnies on a tightrope at the Cirque de Paris.

"Jugglers and acrobats and clowns – oh, my!" Minnie cries.

Millie sees nine bunnies at the Métro.

"Next stop, Champ de Mars!" Minnie says.

THE EIFFEL TOWER

"We've got the last 10 bunnies," Minnie says.

"Now it's time to head back to the hotel!"

Minnie has a lot of bows to make

and not a lot of time to make them!

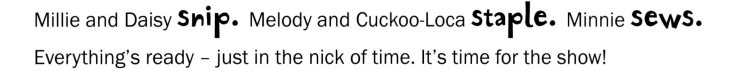

Millie and Daisy **snip.** Melody and Cuckoo-Loca **staple.** Minnie **sews.**
Everything's ready – just in the nick of time. It's time for the show!

Minnie and her helpers hop into a taxi –

and Penguini the Magnificent is right behind them!

He's been looking all over Paris for his bunnies!

At the show,

Daisy gathers the models.

Minnie ties on the bows.

Cuckoo-Loca crosses her wings for good luck.

Minnie's new bows are perfectly Parisian – made
from souvenirs she gathered on the great bunny chase.

"Minnie, you are the
crème de la crème
of the bow business!"
cheers Cuckoo Chanel.

"Oh, my!" says Minnie with a smile.
"Merci bow-coup, Paris!"